Chasing Manet

by Tina Howe

A SAMUEL FRENCH ACTING EDITION

SAMUEL FRENCH

FOUNDED 1830

NEW YORK HOLLYWOOD LONDON TORONTO

SAMUELFRENCH.COM

ISBN 978-0-573-69756-2   Printed in U.S.A.   #29197

MUSIC USE NOTE

Licensees are solely responsible for obtaining formal written permission from copyright owners to use copyrighted music in the performance of this play and are strongly cautioned to do so. If no such permission is obtained by the licensee, then the licensee must use only original music that the licensee owns and controls. Licensees are solely responsible and liable for all music clearances and shall indemnify the copyright owners of the play and their licensing agent, Samuel French, Inc., against any costs, expenses, losses and liabilities arising from the use of music by licensees.

IMPORTANT BILLING AND CREDIT REQUIREMENTS

All producers of *CHASING MANET must* give credit to the Author of the Play in all programs distributed in connection with performances of the Play, and in all instances in which the title of the Play appears for the purposes of advertising, publicizing or otherwise exploiting the Play and/or a production. The name of the Author *must* appear on a separate line on which no other name appears, immediately following the title and *must* appear in size of type not less than fifty percent of the size of the title type.

CHASING MANET was first produced by Primary Stages (Casey Childs, executive producer) in New York City on May 24, 2009. The performance was directed by Michael Wilson, with sets by Tony Straiges, costumes by David C. Wollard, lighting by Howell Binkley, and sound by John Gromada. The production stage manager was Susie Cordon. The cast was as follows:

CATHERINE	Jane Alexander
RENNIE	Lynn Cohen
HENRY, MAURICE, CAPTAIN	David Margulies
CHARLES, GABE, STEWARD	Robert Christopher Riley
ESPERANZA, ANGELICA, SAVIANA, MARIE CLAIRE	Vanessa Aspillaga
RITA, IRIS	Julie Halston
ROYAL, MARVIN, SHERWOOD	Jack Gilpin

CHARACTERS

(In order of appearance)

HENRY – A patient who cries for help

SAVIANA – A patient who makes strange noises

IRIS – A patient with Alzheimer's disease

CATHERINE SARGENT – A prominent painter from Boston who's legally blind and suffers from depression, among other ailments, 80s

CHARLES – Nurse and PT instructor, African American, a man with a past, 30s-40s

ESPERANZA – Catherine and Rennie's Hispanic nurse, 30s

ROYAL LOWELL – Catherine's son, a professor in the English Department at Columbia, 50s

RENNIE WALTZER – Catherine's new roommate, a lively Jewish woman in the early stages of dementia, wheelchair bound due to crippling arthritis, 80s

RITA – Rennie's daughter, 50s

GABE – Rita's husband, African American, 40s-50s

MAURICE – Rennie's brother, 70s

MARVIN – Rennie's son, 50s

ANGELICA – Marvin's Hispanic wife, 40s

SHERWOOD – A patient, the proverbial dirty old man

MARIE CLAIRE – The French arts and crafts instructor, 40s

STEWARD – From Trinidad, 30s

CAPTAIN OF THE QE2 – A charming Englishman, 60s

ACTOR BREAKDOWN

4 Actresses:

CATHERINE SARGENT, 60s-70s

RENNIE WALTZER, 60s-70s

ESPERANZA, ANGELICA, SAVIANA, MARIE CLAIRE (Hispanic) 30s-40s

IRIS, RITA, 50s

3 Actors:

CHARLES, GABE, STEWARD, (African American) 30s-40s

ROYAL, MARVIN, SHERWOOD, 50s

HENRY, MAURICE, CAPTAIN OF THE QE2, 60s

A NOTE ABOUT THE SET

There should be something dreamlike about Mount Airy, a transparency at the edges of the ceiling and walls so the rooms and hallways drift into each other. One should have the feeling it could float away at any moment.

for Quincy Howe, my remarkable brother

ACT I

Scene One

(The Mount Airy Nursing Home in Riverdale, New York. It's an overcast morning in March, mid-1980s. We see the main hall where **HARRY** *and* **IRIS** *are lined up in their wheelchairs, as well as Catherine's drab room, which is furnished with two beds, two dressers, two closets, four uncomfortable chairs, a door leading to the bathroom, and a window overlooking the park. But like everything else in the place, nothing is quite moored to the ground. A large print of Manet's "Luncheon on the Grass" floats over* **CATHERINE** *'s bed, where she lies with her face to the wall. Her roommate's dead body has just been removed.* **CHARLES** *is remaking the bed as* **ESPERANZA** *packs up her personal belongings.)*

CHARLES. *(shaking out the top sheet)* Up, up and awaaaay...

ESPERANZA. She had a good life, that Miss Clara...Loving children, a pack of grandkids and what about that head of hair? I've never seen anything like it! *(indicating with her hands)* Out to here! Like a cloud of cotton candy! And *brave?* What that poor woman endured...

IRIS. LOOK OUT FOR THAT KILOMETER, IT'S COMING RIGHT AT US! UH OH, THERE GO THE SWIMMERS...

*(**ROYAL LOWELL**, Catherine's professorial looking son, 50s, appears.)*

(making a bee line for him with lurid kissing sounds) Arthur, finally! Where have you been, you naughty hootenanny, you! Get over here and give us a nice piss!

9

ROYAL. *(gingerly backing away)* Excuse me, but I believe you've mistaken me for someone else.

IRIS. *(lunging at him)* Puffin, Luffin, my Muffin man! Come whirl me into butter!

ESPERANZA. *(restraining her)* Iris, honey, this isn't your brother, it's Miss Catherine's son!

IRIS. *(suddenly vicious, trying to hit him)* WHAT THE HELL DID YOU DO TO SPANKY PANTS, YOU BASTARD? Bastard, bastard...bastard.

ESPERANZA. Sweetheart, *please!* If you can't be nice to our visitors, I'll have to take you back to your room. Is that what you want on a lovely morning like this? Where's my sweet Iris-cita, hmm? Where did my little girl go?

(IRIS abruptly wheels down the hall and out of sight. A slight silence as they watch her go.)

ESPERANZA. Sorry about that.

ROYAL. No harm done.

ESPERANZA. Why Mr. Lowell, you shaved off your beard!

ROYAL. That was weeks ago.

ESPERANZA. Now I can see your face.

ROYAL. Which is why all my students are begging me to grow it back. So, how is she?

ESPERANZA. *(lowering her voice)* Clara Trigger died.

ROYAL. She *died?*

ESPERANZA. Early this morning.

ROYAL. Clara Trigger...

ESPERANZA. She's at peace now. God bless her soul.

ROYAL. Mother must be delirious, she hated Clara Trigger! The woman cried night and day through that creepy voice box of hers. OK, Esmeralda, I'd better get over there and face the music.

ESPERANZA. *Esperanza!* How many times do I have to tell you? My name is *Esperanza!*

ROYAL. Right, right, sorry.

> *(entering to see* **CATHERINE** *lying on her side facing the wall)*

Well, you must be a happy camper! You've got the whole place to yourself again. What do you do to your roommates, anyway? None of them lasts more than a few months with you. It must be your ribald sense of humor that wears them down. *(giving her a chaste peck on top of her head)* Hi Mum, it's me Royal, your favorite son, your only son... How have you been?

CATHERINE. *(face still to the wall)* Out! Out! I want out.

ROYAL. So...you're queen of the roost again.

CATHERINE. *(in a whisper)* O.U.T.! Out!

ROYAL. *(waving towards the empty bed)* Did she, um...you know...die in the room?

> *(***CATHERINE** *sits up, her great mane of white hair tumbling around her shoulders. She was clearly a beauty in her day, but goes out of her way to look as unkempt as possible.)*

CATHERINE. *(squinting at him)* You're different. Come closer so I can see you.

> *(He does.)*

CATHERINE. Your beard's gone!

ROYAL. Sabine insisted.

CATHERINE. Thank God! I hated that thing! It looked like a dying rodent clinging to your face.

ROYAL. Thanks, Mum. Thanks a lot.

CATHERINE. *(with a sigh)* Poor Royal...beauty was never your strong suit. How *is* Sabine? I haven't seen her in so long I've forgotten what she looks like.

ROYAL. Join the group. Ever since her mother moved to California, I'm lucky if I see her once a year.

CATHERINE. She must be a teenager by now.

ROYAL. She just turned 35!

CATHERINE. *35?* Good God, how long have I been here?

ROYAL. Just over a year.

CATHERINE. You mean, *decade!* Look at me... I'm a ruin, a broken down old crone.

ROYAL. Sabine's mother is on her fourth husband, if you can believe it. Well, that's a novelist for you.

CATHERINE. Don't you ever think of remarrying?

ROYAL. Once was enough, thank you very much.

CATHERINE. *(with a sigh)* Poor Royal.

ROYAL. Why do you always call me "Poor Royal" and then sigh like that?

CATHERINE. Because you lack courage.

ROYAL. Thanks, Mum. Thanks a lot.

CATHERINE. Why dissemble? Honesty is the best policy.

ROYAL. But there's a difference between honesty and cruelty.

CATHERINE. That's a good one... *You* talking about cruelty! *(She laughs bitterly.)*

ROYAL. Where were we? Ah yes...Clara Trigger! Did the poor thing die *here?* I mean, right under your nose?

CATHERINE. Of course she died here! Where else would she die? In the Grand Ballroom of the Plaza Hotel?

ROYAL. I just thought she might have been taken to the hospital.

CATHERINE. Taken to the *hospital?* Honestly Royal, for a college professor you can be awfully dumb sometimes!

ROYAL. Yeah, well, it's an occupational hazard.

CATHERINE. *Nursing homes* are where you're taken to die, in case you've forgotten!

ROYAL. Right, right.

CATHERINE. And by your own son, if you please.

ROYAL. Whatever you say.

CATHERINE. And not even in Boston, but whisked off to some hell hole in the *Bronx!*

ROYAL. Riverdale, *Riverdale!*

CATHERINE. Where they have that vulgar cheer. *(She emits a lurid Bronx cheer.)*

ROYAL. I wanted you nearby.

CATHERINE. Close enough to pop in on, *if* the spirit moves you. *(another cheer)* Which it never does! *(and two more)*

ROYAL. You know what my schedule is like!

CATHERINE. Out! Out! I want out!

ROYAL. Not that again.

CATHERINE. Yes, that again and I'm *getting* out, thank you very much!

ROYAL. And how do you think you'll make it out the door?

CATHERINE. *Vouloir c'est pouvoir!*

ROYAL. *But you're legally blind!*

CATHERINE. I can still distinguish between light and dark.

ROYAL. If someone's shining a flashlight in your eyes!

CATHERINE. And make out large shapes.

ROYAL. If you crash into them!

CATHERINE. My eyesight's fine! Just a bit blurry on some edges.

ROYAL. And what about your heart condition, migraines, and depression?

CATHERINE. Oh, stop being such a stick in the mud! I want out and I'm getting out, so there!

(slight silence)

ROYAL. Was it difficult?

CATHERINE. Was *what* difficult?

ROYAL. *(pointing at the empty bed)* Clara Trigger's death.

CATHERINE. How would I know?

ROYAL. I mean, was it difficult for *you?*

CATHERINE. What a silly question. *She* was the one who died, not me!

ROYAL. Was it difficult for you to...you know...*watch?*

CATHERINE. You mean did she come staggering towards me, sputtering in that fog horn voice of hers, "BUT I WAS SUPPOSED TO BE THE EXCEPTION! I WAS SUPPOSED TO BE THE EXCEPTION!"

ROYAL. *(laughing)* Mum!

CATHERINE. For once in her life, the old cry baby didn't make a peep. She died in her sleep, clutching onto that ridiculous "Happy Hundredth Birthday" telegram President Reagan sent her – lucky stiff!

ROYAL. I'm really sorry. You weren't supposed to end up like this.

CATHERINE. Then get me out of here!

ROYAL. How many times do I have to tell you? I wish I could, but my hands are tied.

CATHERINE. *(erupting out of bed and lurching towards the door)* FUCK YOU! JUST...FUCK YOU!

ROYAL. Hey, where do you think you're going?

CATHERINE. *(heading into the hall)* To find someone who can!

RENNIE. *(down the hall)* What's the room number again?

RITA. Three twelve. It must be at the end of the hall.

MAURICE. Great! A mile from the nurse's station!

RITA. If she needs a nurse, she'll ring.

(CATHERINE *crashes into* RENNIE WALTZER, *80s, being wheeled down the hall by her daughter,* RITA. *Though suffering from early dementia, she looks great in a nice dress and matching hat. Her younger brother,* MAURICE *is at her side.* CATHERINE *and* RENNIE *scream as...*)

RITA.	MAURICE.
Look out! Look out!	Jesus Christ! Watch where you're going!

ROYAL. *(running after* CATHERINE*)* I'm so sorry. Are you alright, Mum?

CATHERINE. NO, I'M NOT ALRIGHT, YOU BLITHERING IDIOT!

ROYAL. Come on, let's get you back to bed.

(*ROYAL leads her, limping, back to her room.*)

CATHERINE. *(whirling away from him)* Hands off!

(*ROYAL backs away as she struggles into bed, as* **RENNIE** *and her family proceed up the hall.*)

RENNIE. What's the room number again?

RITA. Three twelve. I asked for a room overlooking the park!

MAURICE. So far, so good!

(*RITA, RENNIE and MAURICE enter.*)

RITA. Here we are!

MAURICE. This can't be right!

RENNIE. What a nice hotel!

ROYAL. Can I help you?

(*An awkward silence.* **ESPERANZA** *suddenly appears.*)

ESPERANZA. *(to* **CATHERINE***)* Well, it looks like your new roommate has arrived.

RENNIE. *(excited)* Roommate? I didn't know we'd have roommates.

RITA. Excuse me, but is this room 312?

ROYAL & ESPERANZA. Yes!

RITA. But we asked for a single.

RENNIE. The more the merrier!

(**CATHERINE** *emits a hollow laugh.*)

ESPERANZA. I'm afraid there are no single rooms available at the moment.

RENNIE. *(waving to* **CATHERINE***)* Hi, I'm Rennie! What's your name?

MAURICE. I'm going to the front desk.

RENNIE. I'm Rennie, short for Ramona.

RITA. No, Ma. Ramona was your *mother*!

MAURICE. *(exiting)* This is an outrage!

(A bell rings down the hall.)

RENNIE. Room service!

ESPERANZA. Excuse me, I've got to answer that call. *(She exits.)*

CATHERINE. *(gleefully)* Another inmate just kicked the bucket! Welcome to The Mount Airy Funeral Home!

(She hums the funeral march.)

ROYAL. Don't mind her, she's been going through a rough patch. Come on, Mum, behave yourself!

RENNIE. Push me closer to the window, Reets. I want to check out the...check out the...what's it called?

RITA. *(pushing her closer)* The *view!*

RENNIE. Right, the *view!* *(peering out the window)* I love it, I love it! We're right over the water!

ROYAL. Water? What water?

RITA. *(sotto voce to* **ROYAL***)* The poor thing's in her own world. One minute she's at the beach with her dead husband and the next she's up in a tree house having a tea party with her dolls. That's why we had to bring her here. *(to* **RENNIE***)* Look at that lovely park down there, Ma. It's perfect for picnics. Once it gets warm we'll bring wine and cheese and have a high old time. Speaking of which, I'm coming by tomorrow to take you to that lovely new Italian restaurant Gabe and I just discovered.

ROYAL. *(heading for the door)* Well, I've got to get going. I teach a class in an hour.

RITA. You're a *teacher?* I used to teach seventh grade! Where do you teach?

ROYAL. Columbia.

RENNIE.	**RITA.**
Didn't Morty go to Columbia?	Our cousin Morty went to Columbia!

ROYAL. Small world.

CATHERINE. Royal has an endowed chair in the English department.

RENNIE. Your name is *Royal*?

CATHERINE. Royal Sargent. Lang Professor of poetry.

RENNIE. *Royal Sargent…* I love that brand!

CATHERINE. The poor thing can't write it, so he teaches it. Which seems pointless to me, since poets are born, not made.

ROYAL. Nice, Mum…very nice!

(**RENNIE** *sings the old Royal pudding jingle.*)

(**ALL** *look at her in amazement.*)

CATHERINE. *(sitting up)* I remember that jingle! They used to play it on the radio a thousand years ago.

(**CATHERINE AND RENNIE** *sing it together.*)

RITA.	ROYAL.
(applauding) Bravo! Bravo!	*(applauding)* Brava! Brava!

RENNIE. *(bowing)* Thank you, thank you. Thank you very much. *(pause)* Where were we?

RITA. Talking about her son who teaches poetry at Columbia.

RENNIE. Poetry! Oh, I love poetry! Sing something for us!

RITA. He's not a performing seal, Ma!

ROYAL. Well, let's see… I'm working on a book about Yeats…

CATHERINE. *Still?* How long has it been now? Ten years? Fifteen?

RENNIE. *(clapping her hands)* Begin, begin! I love pottery!

ROYAL. "A mermaid found a swimming lad…"

(**MAURICE** *reenters the room.*)

RITA. Ssssh, he's reciting Yeats. He teaches at Columbia.

MAURICE. What do you know, our cousin Morty went to Columbia!

ROYAL. "A mermaid found a swimming lad,
    Picked him for her own,
    Pressed her body to his body,
    Laughed; and plunging down
    Forgot in cruel happiness
    That even lovers drown."

*(Pause, then **RENNIE**'s family applauds as:)*

CATHERINE. *(acidic)* Well, that was nice and gay!

MAURICE. I'm afraid that nurse was right. They don't have any singles at the moment, so this is it until something opens up.

RITA. I'm sorry, Ma.

RENNIE. What are you talking about? I couldn't be happier! I've got a lovely room, a lovely roommate and a lovely view of the…of the…you know… I'm going to take a little nap and then go for a swim. *(to **CATHERINE**)* I'm sorry, I'm afraid I forgot your name. I'm Rennie, short for Ramona. Maybe you'd like to join Herschel and me for a quick dip after lunch. *(trying to get out of her wheelchair)* "Last one in is a rotten egg!"

End of Scene

Scene Two

(April. Two weeks later, 10 a.m. Physical therapy class in the sun room. One by one, five patients enter in their wheelchairs and form a circle. They include: **RENNIE,** *wearing a lovely antique shawl over a nice dress;* **HENRY,** *in a tattered bathrobe;* **SAVIANA,** *in a bizarre Victorian peignoir and wool hat;* **IRIS,** *dressed in a cacophony of mis-matched clothes; and* **SHERWOOD,** *the proverbial dirty old man, dressed accordingly.* **CHARLES,** *their instructor comes striding into their midst.)*

CHARLES. Good morning, boys and girls. How are we doing today?

(They respond simultaneously as **CHARLES** *tries to quiet them.)*

RENNIE. I always loved camp when I was a girl. My poor sister Rachel was so homesick she never lasted more than a week. But not me! Everyone wanted me on their *tassel! (as...)*

SHERWOOD. I'm feeling particularly frisky today and was hoping one of you lovely young ladies might join me for a little roll in the hay...bang in the barn...delight in the dairy... *(as...)*

HENRY. Help! Help! Someone help me please! I need help! Help! Help! Please help me! Help! Help! Someone help me please. I need help! *(as...)*

*(***SAVIANA** *makes sounds like a car alarm as...)*

IRIS. I don't like your face or your sparkle johns! Just look at those white snakes! They're pouring out of your thingamajig! Uuuuggh, I'm going to throw up! *(as...)*

CHARLES. *(waving his arms)* Alright...quiet down! One at a time... *One at a time!* I'm trying to run a class here. I said, QUIET! DOWN! Keep this up and I'm walking out of here. Did you hear me? I SAID: I AM LEAVING THE PREMISES! *(eventually overpowering them)* PEOPLE, PEOPLE...*PLEASE!*

*(Dead silence. **CATHERINE** suddenly staggers into the
room as Oedipus – hair flying, fists in her wildly rouged
eyes. Everyone screams.)*

CATHERINE. *(in a dramatic voice)* Enter blind Oedipus.
"Where shall I find harbor in this world? My voice is
hurled far on a dark wind."

CHARLES. "O cloud of night, never to be turned away."

CATHERINE. Good grief, you know the lines!

CHARLES. Of course I know the lines. I was a professional
actor!

RENNIE. I thought I recognized you.

CATHERINE. *(feeling her way across the room to a chair)* Sorry,
I'm late but I had important business to attend to
– fathers to kill and mothers to marry! *(waving at
RENNIE)* Hi there, Jocasta, miss me?

RENNIE. Rennie, Rennie…my name is *Rennie!*

HENRY. Help! Help! Someone help me please! I need help!
Help! Help! Please help me!

CHARLES. HENRY, HENRY, TAKE IT EASY, MAN!

*(**HENRY** starts to cry.)*

(kneeling at his side) You're in physical therapy class now.
You've got the whole rest of the day to be crazy.

IRIS. I for one, prefer asparagus to playing the harmonica.

SHERWOOD. Whereas, I prefer playing with *myself*. Wanna
join me? Do ya, huh? Do ya? Do ya?

CHARLES. OK, people, enough with the fun and games,
let's get started. How about we begin with our…
"Morning Toss"?

*(**SAVIANA** makes whomping noises like a big load of
laundry in a spin cycle.)*

RENNIE. *(clapping her hands)* Morning Toss! Morning Toss!

CHARLES. Let's loosen up those stiff joints. *(producing a
beach ball from behind his back)* You may think this is a
beach ball, but it's actually a piece of molten lava an
enchanting young lady gave me in Hawaii back when

I was young and baaaad! *(wriggling his hips)* Oh yes! If you don't get rid of it fast, it'll burn clear through your hands, just like her sizzling cheating heart! *(tossing it to* **SAVIANA***)* Heads up, baby, throw it to someone else!

RENNIE & ALL. *(waving her arms)* Here, here, throw it to me.

*(**SAVIANA** throws it to **RENNIE** who throws it to **HENRY** who throws it to **SHERWOOD** who throws it to **IRIS** who throws it back to **SHERWOOD** who throws it to **RENNIE** who throws it to **SAVIANA** who throws it to **SHERWOOD** who throws it to **IRIS**.)*

CHARLES. *(as they toss it around)* Nice work! Good job! Keep it up! Heads up, Oedipus. Catch!

*(**IRIS** throws it back to **SHERWOOD** who throws it to **CHARLES** who throws it to **CATHERINE** who holds onto it.)*

Throw the ball, baby!

RENNIE. *(waving her arms)* Here, here! Throw it to me!

*(**CATHERINE** doesn't move.)*

CHARLES. I SAID, "THROW IT!" THAT'S A PIECE OF RED HOT LAVA YOU'VE GOT IN YOUR HANDS!

CATHERINE. Excuse me, but I believe it's inflated *plastic!*

EVERYONE AT ONCE. Here, here, throw it to me! Throw it to me!

CHARLES. Your team mates are waiting!

CATHERINE. Let them wait, this is demeaning. I refuse to play.

CHARLES. My dear Catherine, if you don't use your muscles, they'll atrophy on you. As a licensed physical therapy instructor as well as a golden glove boxer, actor, singer, lifeguard and flight instructor…I am asking you to… Please. Throw. The ball!

RENNIE. *(waving her arms)* Rachel, Rachel, over here!

CATHERINE. How many times do I have to tell you, my name is *Catherine*! I'm *not* your sister Rachel! And how do you expect me to throw it to you if I'm legally blind!

CHARLES. But not deaf, so just aim it in her general direction.

RENNIE. *(chanting throughout)* Here, here… I'm right over here… Oooo hooo… Over here, over here… *(etc.)*

(CATHERINE *runs her hands over the ball, feeling for the spout, finds it, pulls out the stopper and violently pushes all the air out. Everyone gasps.)*

CHARLES. Hey, what do you think you're doing?

RENNIE. Where did the ball go?

CATHERINE. *(waving it at* RENNIE, *now flat as a pancake)* Head's up, Rache! *(throwing it and deliberately missing by a mile)* Catch!

End of Scene

Scene Three

(The end of April. Catherine and Rennie's room. Catherine's side is as spare as ever, but Rennie's explodes with furniture and personal effects – scatter rugs, a chaise longue, an antique chest of drawers, standing lamps, fabulous bedding, mirrors, a blizzard of framed family photographs and a fancy white telephone. It looks as if a boudoir out of House Beautiful has been air-lifted into the room. It's Sunday afternoon around 3:00. **CATHERINE**'s *in bed with her face to the wall.* **RENNIE**'s *all dolled up because she has company which includes* **MAURICE** – *who's in the middle of telling a funny story* – *her son* **MARVIN;** **ANGELICA,** *Maurice's Hispanic wife,* **RITA** *and her African-American husband,* **GABE.***)*

MAURICE. So, after fleeing the earthquakes in New Zealand, they sail to Hawaii, hoping for a better life. Our grandfather steps off the boat, finds an old Jewish tailor and asks, How's business?" The tailor shrugs, saying…

ALL. *(joining in)* "Eh!"

RITA. Jewish market research!

MAURICE. …Which is why he and the family turned around and sailed to San Francisco, arriving just in time for the earthquake of 1906!

(Everyone roars with laughter.)

RITA. Oh, Uncle Maurice, I must have heard that story a million times.

MARVIN. Make that two million, Sis!

MAURICE. *(passing around the platter)* Anyone care for another piece of apricot rugelah?

ANGELICA. No more for me, thanks.

RITA. Eat, eat!

MAURICE. *(taking one)* Melt in your mouth!

GABE. *(patting his stomach)* Keep this up and I'll have to be rushed to the nearest hospital.

RENNIE. *(yelling offstage)* Herschel! You'd better get in here while there's still something left!

RITA. *(sotto voce to the others)* She talks to him all the time now.

MAURICE. What's the harm? It comforts her.

RITA. But he passed away five years ago.

MAURICE. It has nothing to do with time.

MARVIN. Damn lung cancer!

RITA. What do you expect? He smoked two packs a day!

MAURICE. Can't we change the subject?

MARVIN. *(eyeing **CATHERINE**, whispering)* What *is* it with her? She's always in bed with her face to the wall.

GABE. *(also whispering)* Wait 'til we're her age, we'll probably be worse!

RITA. Speak for yourself.

MAURICE. *(gazing at **CATHERINE**'s Manet print)* That painting looks so familiar.

MARVIN. It's a Renoir!

MAURICE. I'd recognize his work anywhere! Oh, I love Renoir!

CATHERINE. *(turning to face them)* Manet.

RITA. The fellow who did the water lilies!

RENNIE. Water lilies?

CATHERINE. That was Monet.

RENNIE. I don't see any water lilies.

RITA. No, Ma, we're talking about another painting.

ANGELICA. I *love* Manet's water lilies!

CATHERINE. *Monet* painted the water lilies, not *Manet!*

MAURICE. Monet, Manet...I always mix them up!

MARVIN. Manet, Monet, what's the difference?

CATHERINE. *(sitting up)* The difference, sir, is that Monet, like Rembrandt, came at the end of his age and summed it up. He took Impressionism as far as it could go. Manet, on the other hand, was Impressionism's bad boy. He was more interested in shocking the bourgeoisie than refining the form. When this painting appeared in the Salon de Refusés in 1863, it caused a riot.

(All gaze at it, transfixed.)

MARVIN. No wonder! That woman is buck naked!

CATHERINE. It wasn't the fact of her nakedness that was so shocking, but its implausibility. Women don't *do* that! Manet had no interest in depicting an actual event, but an imagined one. Placing a naked woman in a public place sounded the call for artistic freedom, telling the artist he could paint not only what he wanted, but *how*. That bemused woman tore down four centuries of classical tradition, paving the way for what we now refer to as modern art. Which is why it's never left my side, as a reminder of what a feisty young painter can do!

(A brief silence. One by one they all burst into applause and drift over to **CATHERINE**'s *side of the room.)*

MAURICE. Whoa!

RITA. That was incredible!

MARVIN. You really know your art history!

MAURICE. Very impressive!

GABE. *Most* impressive!

ANGELICA. Thank you so much!

RENNIE. Wheel me closer, Reets.

*(***RITA*** wheels her closer until they're all gazing up at the painting.)*

MAURICE. "It wasn't the fact of her nakedness that was so shocking, but its *implausibility*." Were you a professor like your son?

CATHERINE. No, a painter.

ALL. A *painter?*

RENNIE. *(yelling offstage)* Herschel, she's a painter!

MAURICE. Wait a minute, isn't your last name Sargent?

RITA. Oh. My. God!

GABE. *(grabbing* **RITA**'s *arm)* My God, my God, my God…

ANGELICA. Catch me before I faint!

MAURICE. You wouldn't happen to be related to the great portrait painter, John Singer Sargent, would you?

CATHERINE. As a matter of fact, I am. He was a cousin.

MAURICE. Whoa!

GABE. Nice! Very nice!

MARVIN. Holy shit…

ANGELICA. You can say that again!

MARVIN. *Holy shit!*

RITA. Did you hear that, Ma?

RENNIE. What's his name again?

RITA & ANGELICA. John Singer Sargent.

MAURICE. Only the greatest American portrait painters who ever lived!

RENNIE. *I'm rooming with a celebrity! I'm rooming with a celebrity!*

RITA. Easy, Ma, easy!

RENNIE. *(to* **CATHERINE***)* I met Milton Berle once.

MARVIN. You didn't meet him, you just saw him on the street.

(*Silence as they all stare at* **CATHERINE** *with awe.*)

RENNIE. Are you famous too?

CATHERINE. *Infamous* is more like it.

RENNIE. *(in a whisper)* Did you paint yourself in the nude?

RITA. Ma!

CATHERINE. Wouldn't you like to know.

RENNIE. I love it, I love it!

RITA. It's none of our business.

RENNIE. Did you paint *other* people in the nude?

RITA. Don't mind her.

RENNIE. Did you paint *men* in the nude?

RITA. Stop it!

RENNIE. Did you paint their…*(laughing raucously)* you know whats…

(**RITA** *slaps her hand over* **RENNIE***'s mouth.*)

CATHERINE. Their "you know whats" and their "Don't look nows!" But my real focus was on the female body, mine included... I was a Modernist.

RITA & GABE. *(impressed)* A Modernist...

CATHERINE. Manet started the ball rolling by putting a female nude in a public place, the next step was to paint the woman *inside* the nude. And who better to do it than another woman?

MAURICE & ANGELICA. "The woman *inside* the nude..."

CATHERINE. Her *inner* wardrobe, so to speak...her terrors and desires.

RITA.   **ANGELICA.**
Whoaaaaa!   Yesssss!

RENNIE. *(starting to unbutton her dress)* Oh, paint me! Paint me!

CATHERINE. Dream on!

RITA. Ma!

ANGELICA. Is there some place we could see your work?

CATHERINE. The Boston Museum of Fine Arts, the Clark, the Hirshhorn, the Phillips Collection and the Modern, plus a bunch of museums in Europe, South America and Asia.

GABE & MAURICE. *(gasping in awe)* Wow...

(Silence as they gaze at her out of new eyes.)

MARVIN. *(pulling a chair up to her bed)* My son Elliot is also an artist. Not a painter like you, but boy does he have an eye.

RITA. Ohhh, you should see his stuff!

MAURICE. He heads up the design team of one of Jersey's top advertising firms!

RITA. The best! The best!

(The others gather around her as well.)

GABE. And not just his print ads, but his TV work as well!

RITA. You should see the commercial he did for one of our local furriers...

ANGELICA. Unbelievable!

RITA. He got access to these live minks, which he flew over to Venice.

CATHERINE. I've never worn fur in my life.

GABE. With an ace camera crew.

CATHERINE. It harkens back to the Stone Age, if you ask me!

RITA. Then he got these *comedia del arte* masks...

ANGELICA. Tied them to their faces...

RITA. Piled them into a gondola...

GABE. And got this incredible footage of them floating down the Grand Canal...at night!

RITA. With all the lights of the city shimmering in their fur.

MAURICE. As Vivaldi's "Gloria" played in the background.

(He hums the opening melody. They all join in in full-throated chorus.)

CATHERINE. Who on earth would want to watch rodents in a *gondola*?

ANGELICA. They looked like Renaissance princes...

(CATHERINE shudders.)

It was like something out of a dream. Marvin went out and bought me a chinchilla wrap the very next day!

CATHERINE. Good grief!

MAURICE. He won every award in the business! Including Best Commercial of 1979!

RENNIE. Who are you talking about? Who are you talking about?

MARVIN, RITA, & ANGELICA. Elliot!

RENNIE. Rachel's little boy!

MARVIN. No, *my* little boy! And he's not so little anymore! He's 32 years old!

MAURICE. Speaking of Rachel, she's flying over next month.

RENNIE. Rachel! Rachel!

MAURICE. *(to* **CATHERINE***)* Rachel's our older sister. Her husband's an M.P. He was knighted two years ago! She's been living in London so long, she's more British than the Queen herself.

MARVIN. We call her Lady Rachel because she's become very grand. You should hear her accent. *(putting it on)* "I say! Can I interest anyone in a spot of tea?"

MAURICE. *(following suit:)* "It's frightfully bracing and excellent for the collywobbles!"

(All laugh.)

RENNIE. She's taking me out to lunch tomorrow.

RITA. No, *I'm* taking you out for lunch tomorrow. Rachel isn't flying over for a month or so.

MARVIN. *(to* **CATHERINE***)* She's a champion gardener. You should see her roses…

ANGELICA. *(holding her hand three feet over the floor)* This high!

GABE. Incredible!

ANGELICA. In the most brilliant colors you've ever seen!

GABE. They look like tropical birds! You expect them to fly right off their stems. *(He makes tropical bird calls)*

RITA. *(to* **RENNIE***)* And she's taking *you* to the New York Botanical Garden when she comes!

MARVIN. Did you hear that? When Rachel comes she's taking *you* to the New York Botanical Garden!

RENNIE. *(clapping her hands)* Goodie, goodie, I love binoculars!

(slight silence)

MARVIN. *(offering a platter of food to* **CATHERINE***)* Where are my manners? Would you care from some rugelah or a prune danish? A new bakery just opened up down the street.

ANGELICA. Forget it! He's over there three times a day!

CATHERINE. *(softly)* Out! Out! I want out!

MAURICE. I can't imagine it's very pleasant here for someone as intelligent as you.

GABE. *(to* **RITA***)* When I get to be that age, I'm going to off myself!

RITA. *(swatting him)* Gabe?!

GABE. And I'm taking you with me.

RITA. *Honey?!*

CATHERINE. *(grabbing his hand)* Out, out, I want out! Out, out, I want out!

(slight pause)

RENNIE. *(gleefully imitating her)* Out, out, I want out! Out, out, I want out!

RITA & MARVIN. *Ma?*

CATHERINE. Out!

(Rennie's family looks at them not knowing whether to laugh or not.)

End of Scene

Scene Four

(Later that night. The shades are up, moonlight dapples the room. Both women are in bed. **CATHERINE**'s *snoring lustily. She starts to thrash in the throes of a nightmare. Her snores turn into deep throated moans and guttural cries, making her sound like a man.* **RENNIE** *sits up in bed.)*

RENNIE. HERSCHEL, WAKE UP! YOU'RE HAVING A NIGHTMARE!

*(***CATHERINE**'s *cries become more anguished.)*

HANG ON, BABY, I'M COMING, I'M COMING!

*(***RENNIE** *gets out of bed and onto her walker.)*

Ohhh, ahhhh…everything hurts! My neck, my shoulders, my arms and legs. Always the legs, always the damn legs… Ow! Ow! Ow! Easy does it… Take your time, Ren… No sudden moves… You don't want to break any bones… *(making her way over to* **CATHERINE** *and shaking her)* WAKE UP HERSCHEL, IT'S ME! YOU'RE HAVING ANOTHER NIGHTMARE!

CATHERINE. *(waking with a piercing cry)* André?

RENNIE. Herschel?

CATHERINE. Where are you?

RENNIE. Wake up!

CATHERINE. Darling?

RENNIE. Sweetheart?

CATHERINE. Yoo hoo…

RENNIE. It's me…

CATHERINE. Are you there?

RENNIE. Rennie…

CATHERINE. Say something.

RENNIE. *(climbing into her bed and nuzzling her)* Your little puddle duck!

CATHERINE. *(at the top of her lungs)* HELP! HELP! HELP! HELP!

(ESPERANZA *rushes in and turns on the light.*)

ESPERANZA. Ladies, ladies, what's going on in here?

CATHERINE.

I was sound asleep when this maniac woke me up, babbling about Herschel. The next thing I knew she was in bed with me!

RENNIE.

Herschel was having a nightmare, I was trying to wake him up and suddenly *she* was in his bed!

ESPERANZA. Please, please, one at a time.

CATHERINE. I was sleeping, for once…and *she* attacked me.

RENNIE. He was having a nightmare.

ESPERANZA. *Who* was having a nightmare?

RENNIE. Herschel! Every night another nightmare! The moaning and screaming! He's driving me crazy!

CATHERINE. It's impossible to sleep in this mad house, but that's a nursing home for you!

RENNIE. Nursing home, what are you talking about? This is a *hotel*!

CATHERINE. A *hotel*?! (*She bursts out laughing.*)

RENNIE. Yes.

ESPERANZA. (*to* CATHERINE) Alright, dear, that's enough!

CATHERINE. (*laughing harder and harder*) A *hotel*?

RENNIE. The four star Mount Airy Hotel!

CATHERINE. (*weeping with laughter*) The four star Mount Airy *Hotel!* Ohhhh, that's the funniest thing I've ever heard!

ESPERANZA. (*gently to* RENNIE) Don't listen to her. It's whatever *you* want it to be. Hotel, B&B, spa

CATHERINE. (*drying her eyes*) A *hotel*…

ESPERANZA. Ranch, cabana, spaceship…

CATHERINE. Ohhh, that felt good!

ESPERANZA. (*to* CATHERINE) OK, Sweetheart, now tell me what happened.

CATHERINE. OK, *Sweetheart,* I was flying across the Bosporus in a two seater plane with André Malraux when we suddenly started to fall. As I lunged for the controls, he turned into this enormous...speckled...bird... He told me to climb on his back. I did and as we were about to fly out the door, *she* attacked me...

ESPERANZA. Who's André Malraux?

CATHERINE. A famous French writer and intellectual and one of my old lovers.

RENNIE. What did you do with Herschel?

CATHERINE. *(sotto voce)* Nothing, since he's been dead for the past five years.

RENNIE. He shares the room with me.

CATHERINE. Along with the King and Queen of England.

ESPERANZA. Ladies, ladies!

RENNIE. *(starting to cry)* I want Herschel, I want Herschel!

ESPERANZA. There, there, let's get you back to bed.

(ESPERANZA helps her.)

RENNIE. *(groaning all the way)* Ow! Ow! My legs, my legs!

CATHERINE.	RENNIE.
Out, out, I want out!	Ohhhhh... Ahhhh...
Out! Out! Out! Out!	Aaaaaaa...

ESPERANZA. There we go, sweetheart, back to beddy-byes.

RENNIE. *(weepy)* I want to go home, I want to go home!

CATHERINE. *(singing)* "Home, home on the range, where the deer and the artichoke play..."

ESPERANZA. *(shaking out pills from a bottle)* OK, my darlings...

CATHERINE. *(continues singing)* "...where seldom is heard an intelligent word..."

ESPERANZA. ...that's enough. I gotta go – my own little chicks are waiting for me at home. I'm giving you something to help you get back to sleep. Here, take this, it will calm you down. I hear you have a big day tomorrow, Rennie. Your daughter's taking you out to some fancy new restaurant.

(*handing her a pill*)

(**RENNIE** *swallows it.*)

ESPERANZA. Good girl. (*and one to* **CATHERINE**) And one for you, Precious.

CATHERINE. "Precious?" Since when am I "Precious" to you? My name is *Catherine*, if you don't mind! (*putting the pill in her mouth, then spitting it out*)

ESPERANZA. Now I don't want to hear another peep out of either of you, do you hear? (*turning out the light*) Life would be so much easier if you tried to get along.

(*A silence.*)

(**CATHERINE** *puts a pillow over her face and screams.*)

RENNIE. What was that?

CATHERINE. The sound of a drowning woman! I want out and I'm getting out!

RENNIE. You are?

CATHERINE. *I can't take this anymore!* (*looking under her pillow*) Where is it?

RENNIE. What?

CATHERINE. (*pulling it out*) My passport!

RENNIE. (*loud*) Your *passport?*

CATHERINE. Ssshhh, not so loud!

RENNIE. (*whispering*) Where are you going?

CATHERINE. To Paris.

RENNIE. *Paris?*

CATHERINE. I'm booking passage on the QE2.

RENNIE. *The QE2?* What's that?

CATHERINE. An ocean liner that sails to Europe.

RENNIE. The QE2, of course! Herschel and I have taken it a million times!

CATHERINE. (*in a dramatic whisper*) I'm going to escape!

RENNIE. *Escape?*

CATHERINE. Shhhh!

RENNIE. But it's against the law!

CATHERINE. Law? What law?

RENNIE. I don't know.

CATHERINE. I'm going to slip out of here, board the QE2 and sail to France.

RENNIE. *Why?*

CATHERINE. To join Manet and his impropbable picnic.

RENNIE. But...but...what about me?

CATHERINE. What *about* you?

RENNIE. What will I do?

CATHERINE. Whatever you want.

RENNIE. But I thought we were roommates.

CATHERINE. *Roommates?*

RENNIE. You know...best friends... That we stuck together.
(*silence*)

CATHERINE. (*a light bulb going off*) Wait a minute... Wait. Just. One. Minute. Would you like to come with me?

RENNIE. Come *with* you?

CATHERINE. To Paris! On the QE2! My treat!

RENNIE. Can Herschel come too?

CATHERINE. The more, the merrier!

RENNIE. We love Paris! We went there on our honeymoon. (*showing off her bad French*) "Voulez vous coucher avec môi ce soir?"

CATHERINE. Actually, it would be a big help to have you along. You'd be my seeing eye dog, so to speak. You could bark out directions as I push you around the deck. The blind leading the crippled... I can just see us at the Louvre! "Look for the ramp at the end of the Egyptian wing...atta girl... Now turn to the left... That's it...past the Winged Victory... Slow down, it's coming right up... Et le voilà, my beloved *Le Déjeuner sur l'herbe*! You, me and Manet...! It's brilliant, just *brilliant*! But hold on...do you have a passport?

RENNIE. Thousands of 'em! Wait til I tell Herschel!

CATHERINE. (*all whispered*) But no one else. Promise!

RENNIE. *(doing it)* Cross my heart and hope to die.

CATHERINE. Now I just have to order the tickets and come up with a plan to get us out of here.

End of Scene

Scene Five

*(May. Several days later, around three in the afternoon.
Since Rita's taken Rennie out for lunch, CATHERINE's
spread out on Rennie's chaise, wearing one of her shawls,
her hair pulled up in an elegant Gibson knot. She's talking on the phone with an agent from the Cunard Line,
looking and sounding very grand.)*

CATHERINE. I'd like to book passage on the QE2 depart-
ing New York May 22nd, arriving Le Havre, May 28th.
I trust you still have room to squeeze in a couple of
spry "older" women. *(listening)* Thank God! Yes, a
stateroom for two on the upper deck. With an ocean
view... Mmm... Mmm... Mmm... Mmmmm... Perfect!
That sounds lovely! My companion is in a wheelchair
so we'll need a room that...

*(A distant chorus of patients weeping, braying and
crying for help starts up in the hall.)*

HENRY. Help! Help! Someone help me please! I need help!
Help! Help! Please help me! Help! Help! Someone
help me please. I need help!

IRIS. *(singing)* "Oh my darling, oh my darling, oh my darling, Borderline, you are lost and gone to Poo-Poo, will
you be my concubine?"

CATHERINE. *(covering the receiver)* I'm sorry, I'm calling from
a pay phone on the street and it's a bit noisy! You
know... all the crazy people... *(She laughs.)*

(The chorus gets louder, overlapping.)

HENRY. Help! Help! Someone help me please! I need help!
Help! Help! Please help me! Help! Help! *(as...)*

*(SAVIANA makes sounds like an idling car struggling to
get into gear as...)*

IRIS. I ASKED YOU TO UNSCREW THAT ELEPHANT
FROM THE CEILING! HE'S BLOCKING THE
DAMNED VIEW! *(as...)*

CATHERINE. *(into the phone)* Pardon me for a moment, while I duck into a doorway. *(She rises, puts a pillow over the phone, slowly makes her way out the door and yells down the hall.)*
EXCUSE ME, BUT I'M TRYING TO MAKE A PHONE CALL AND WOULD APPRECIATE IT IF YOU COULD KEEP IT DOWN! I CAN'T HEAR A WORD ANYONE'S SAYING!

(dead silence)

Thank you! Thank you very much! *(feeling her way back into the room and picking up the phone again)* Sorry about that. A man just had a heart attack on the street. An ambulance is on its way. Where were we? *(listening)* Catherine Sargent... Yes, Catherine Sargent, the painter... You saw my retrospective at the Hirshhorn? I'm so flattered... *(listening)* Why, thank you... You made my day, no make that my entire decade! Now about that room we were talking about on the upper deck...$10,847! No problem. I'll have my bank wire it to you immediately. *(to herself)* And coming back? That won't be necessary. Just two one-way tickets... A number where you can reach me? *(She squints at the phone trying to make out the numbers.)* I'm sorry, I'll have to get back to you about that...

*(**ROYAL** suddenly appears at the door carrying a bulging garment bag.)*

ROYAL. My, my don't *you* look grand!

CATHERINE. *Royal?!* *(into the phone)* I'm sorry, but I've got to run. The ambulance just arrived. *(imitating the siren)* I'll call you back when I get home. *(She quickly hangs up, guiltily trying to hide the receiver behind her back.)* How long have you been standing there?

ROYAL. *(remaining at the door)* I just got here, why?

CATHERINE. Something awful just happened!

ROYAL. What?

CATHERINE. I've started hearing things.

ROYAL. What kinds of things?

CATHERINE. Ambulance sirens. *(She imitates it again.)*

ROYAL. Since when?

CATHERINE. Yesterday! It's finally happened. I'm starting to crack up.

> **(CHARLES** *starts playing the piano and singing show tunes down the hall.)*

Well, don't just stand there. Come in and take a load off your feet.

ROYAL. *(looking at* **RENNIE***'s side of the room)* What's going on in here?

CATHERINE. Her husband was in the furniture business.

ROYAL. It makes your side look so…empty.

CATHERINE. Well, as the wise man said: "To be empty is to be full."

ROYAL. "To have little is to possess."

CATHERINE & ROYAL. "And to have plenty is to be perplexed."

ROYAL. Ahh, let's hear it for the good old Yankee penchant for thrift!

CATHERINE. *(in a far away voice)* Hip hip, horay. Hip, hip, hooraaaaaaay.

(slight pause)

ROYAL. Do I hear someone singing show tunes down the hall, or am I cracking up as well?

CATHERINE. It's Charles. He sings for us twice a week. He also acts, boxes and flies planes. God knows why he's working *here!*

ROYAL. *(sitting on her bed)* You look so elegant spread out on that chaise.

CATHERINE. *(gleefully striking a provocative pose)* Who am I?

ROYAL. My demented mother.

CATHERINE. No, Manet's "Olympia."

ROYAL. Since we're on the subject of naked women, there's something I've always wanted to ask. Did you really shed your clothes in public places like her *(pointing at the Manet)* when you left us and ran off to Paris?

CATHERINE. Like I'd tell my *son*!

ROYAL. I've never known if you were actually a loose woman or just *played* one to enhance your image. You know, the brilliant American tease kicking up her heels abroad.

CATHERINE. That's quite a choice you've given me – slut or imposter.

ROYAL. If the shoe fits...

CATHERINE. Well, it doesn't.

ROYAL. I'd like to know because it would help me figure out the wreckage of my own so-called "life."

CATHERINE. *(with a sigh)* Poor Royal.

ROYAL. If only I'd inherited your verve instead of father's moods. Just think if I could disrobe in public...

CATHERINE. Dream on.

ROYAL. No, I envy you. I've always envied you. You never look before you leap. You just run to the top of the precipice, spread out your arms and whoooosh – you're airborne...leaping into the void. *(reciting from "The Second Coming")*

"Turning and turning in the widening gyre

The falcon cannot hear the falconer;

Things falls apart; the centre cannot hold;"

CATHERINE & ROYAL. "Mere anarchy is loosed upon the world..."

CATHERINE. Good old Yeats.

ROYAL. Good old Yeats.

(silence)

CATHERINE. Remember those wonderful skating parties the Cabots used to have when the Charles River froze over?

ROYAL. Where did *that* come from?

CATHERINE. How we'd deck ourselves out in ball gowns, pantaloons and wigs, pretending to be famous characters from the past as we whizzed past the Esplanade.

You were so fast, I thought you'd sprouted wings.

ROYAL. You used to call me your flying swan.

CATHERINE. And didn't the Cabots turn it into a contest one year? I went as Queen Elizabeth, wrapped in a brocade curtain and you went as...

ROYAL & CATHERINE. *(laughing)* Shakespeare! Shakespeare on ice!

CATHERINE. In a ruffled shirt and a hat with a plume!

ROYAL. Skating up and down the Charles, reciting those sonnets...

CATHERINE. You should have seen yourself, zooming under all those bridges, declaiming in a perfect English accent...

ROYAL. "When in disgrace with fortune and men's eyes/I all alone beweep my outcast state/ And trouble deaf heaven with my bootless cries/and look upon myself and curse my fate..."

CATHERINE. You were brilliant, brilliant! And didn't you win first prize for best costume and performance?

ROYAL. I think I did.

CATHERINE. God, it seems like a million years ago!

(**CHARLES** *starts singing a beloved old show tune.*)

CATHERINE. Oh, I love that song!

ROYAL. Me too.

(*They sing along for a few moments, then sigh. Silence.*)

CATHERINE. *(reaching for his hand)* I miss you, Royal, I really do! In the beginning you used to stop by almost every day, and now I see you once a month, if that! You only live 20 minutes away! I thought that's why you snatched me away from my few friends in Boston and plunked me down here. So you could be close by.

ROYAL. *(in a sudden burst of anguish)* How many times do I have to tell you? *I don't have time!* I teach four classes a week, oversee half a dozen Ph.D. theses and am trying to finish my goddamned book on Yeats! I sleep four hours a night if I'm lucky! That fucking university is putting me in my grave! *You're* the one that'll be burying *me!* If I make it through the semester it will be a miracle! A fucking miracle!

CATHERINE. Language, Roy, language!

ROYAL. I thought I had it all figured out... You'd be a stone's throw away so I could visit every day. We'd read poetry together, look through old family photographs, joke about the piles of money father made and lost...

CATHERINE. Who *are* you?

ROYAL. Have picnics in that nice little park.

CATHERINE. Picnics in that nice little park? You've never taken me on a picnic in your entire life!

ROYAL. This is getting scary.

CATHERINE. If *you're* scared, how do you think I feel? *I'm* the one that's been put away.

ROYAL. Please...

CATHERINE. I'm just asking for a few visits now and then.

ROYAL. I don't like endings.

CATHERINE. We all have to go sometime.

ROYAL. Please!

CATHERINE. Awww...

ROYAL. Mum...

CATHERINE. I didn't know you cared.

ROYAL. Of course I care.

CATHERINE. About yourself! You don't want to be left behind because that means you're next.

ROYAL. *(starting to lose it)* Will you stop it, for Christ's sake?! *Just. Stop it!*

CATHERINE. *(taking his hand)* Roy, Roy, you'll get along fine without me... And when it's your turn to go, your students will be there to ease you to the other side... where I'll be waiting. With Daddy and all the old family photographs. We'll have picnics in the park every day, 365 days a year! All your favorites – vichyssoise, cucumber sandwiches, artichoke hearts... *(patting his hand) Or...* we'll be sitting on the topless towers of Ilion, watching the end of the Trojan war as Hector and Achilles slug it out, swords flashing, armor ringing...

ROYAL. OK, OK...

CATHERINE. We're born, we die, that's the deal.

(silence)

ROYAL. *(laying her garment bag on her bed)* So, here are the clothes you wanted me to bring over.

CATHERINE. Thanks, you're an angel!

ROYAL. Though I have to admit I think you're up to something.

CATHERINE. What do you mean?

ROYAL. I never got any announcement about the home putting on a show about famous lovers.

CATHERINE. That's because you never open your mail.

ROYAL. Who are you playing, again?

CATHERINE. Wally Simpson!

ROYAL. That's right, *Wally Simpson! (He bursts out laughing.)*

CATHERINE. What's so funny?

ROYAL. *(laughing harder) You...*as the petite, soigné Duchess of Windsor!

CATHERINE. Well, I'm glad you're enjoying yourself so much. I thought you'd be happy that I was finally entering into the "cultural" events around here.

ROYAL. *(weeping with laughter)* It's just *you...*as *Wally Simpson...!*

CATHERINE. *That's enough! You're being very rude! (hurling a slipper at him and missing by a mile)*

ROYAL. Hey watch it, you could hurt someone!

CATHERINE. That was the point.

ROYAL. OK, fess up, who were you talking to on the phone just now?

CATHERINE. One of my dealers in Europe.

ROYAL. You're plotting something, I know you.

CATHERINE. What? A daring escape to Europe?

RITA. *(appearing at the door with* RENNIE, *stops in her tracks)* Whoops, we seem to be interrupting something.

(CATHERINE *quickly scrambles back to her side of the room.)*

RENNIE. *(to* ROYAL*)* Herschel!

ROYAL. Herschel?

RITA. That's not Herschel, Ma.

RENNIE. Why do you look so familiar?

ROYAL. *(pointing at* CATHERINE*)* I'm her son, Royal!

RITA. Well, I've got to get back home. We're taking Zachie and Zoe to the circus tonight.

RENNIE. Wait till I tell Herschel! He loves the circus!

RITA. No, Ma, I'm taking Zachie and Zoe. We don't have a ticket for you.

RENNIE. What do you mean you don't have a ticket for your father? You know how much he loves the circus!

RITA. Well, I'd better get moving if I want to beat the traffic.

RENNIE. *Herschel, Rita's taking us to the circus!* Herschel! Where is that man? HERSCHEL, HERSCHEL, I WANT HERSCHEL! HERSCHEL, HERSCHEL, I WANT HERSCHEL! *(in a loop)*

RITA. Ma, Ma...where do you think you're going?

(And RENNIE*'s out the door, zig-zagging down the hall where* HENRY *and* IRIS *are dozing in their wheelchairs.)*

CATHERINE. Come on, *do* something, Roy.

ROYAL. Sorry, this ain't my field.

RITA. *(chasing after her)* ? HELP, HELP...MY MOTHER'S RUNNING AMOK!

(RENNIE *crashes into* HENRY.*)*

HENRY. Help, help, help, help...

RENNIE. *(hitting him)* Herschel, Herschel, I want Herschel!

RITA. *(struggling with* RENNIE*)* Ma! Ma!

ESPERANZA. *(suddenly appears and stops* RENNIE*)* Easy, easy... Esperanza's here, Esperanza's going to take care of you! CHARLES, COME QUICK!

(*CHARLES grabs* RENNIE*'s wheelchair and wheels her back into the room.*)

RENNIE. Where's my Herschel, my bushel, my rabbit soufflé? (*breaking down into wracking sobs*)

ROYAL. I've got to get out of here!

CATHERINE. *You've* got to get out of here?

ESPERANZA. Hold still now, be a good girl for Esperanza. (*She administers a shot.*)

CATHERINE. What about *me?* This is where I live, thanks to you...and where I'll die! Give up the ghost! (*yelling after him*) DID YOU HEAR THAT? THIS IS WHERE I'LL MAKE MY EXIT, KICK THE BUCKET, BITE THE DUST, LEAVING YOU ALL SOUL ALONE!

(ROYAL *exits.*)

ESPERANZA. (*approaching her*) Sweetheart, please...

CHARLES. Well, that was quite a...

RITA. Thank you, guys... You were dolls, as always.

CHARLES. Hey, it's our job... Lucky us. Well, I gotta get back to Henry.

ESPERANZA. Wait up, I'll go with you.

(*They exit.* RENNIE*'s fallen asleep with her mouth open. It's suddenly very quiet.*)

RITA. (*full of love*) Just look at her.

CATHERINE. There goes Paris.

(*slower and slower*)

RITA. She was always the picture of health.

CATHERINE. Now you see it, now you don't.

RITA. What happened?

CATHERINE. Darkness descends.

RITA. (*breaking down*) Oh Ma?

CATHERINE. The beasts are coming out of hiding...

RITA. Where are you?

CATHERINE. Shhh! Listen...

RITA. Come back, come back.

CATHERINE. You can hear their muffled footsteps…

RITA. Don't leave me.

CATHERINE. They're coming closer and closer.

RITA. I can't bear it.

  (**CATHERINE** *mimics the ghostly sound.*)

End of Act One

ACT TWO

Scene Seven

(The next day, around noon. The shades are up and sunlight pours into the room. CATHERINE's back in bed with her face to the wall. RENNIE is miraculously back to her old self, all dolled up waiting for Rita to take her to the beauty parlor. She luxuriates in a pool of sunlight which also illuminates Catherine's Manet print.)

RENNIE. *(gazing at it)* I did that once. Took off all my clothes outdoors. Just last week, as a matter of fact... Herschel and I were having a picnic at the lake... It was so hot, I thought I'd croak! A hundred and fifteen in the shade... So I stripped... Then Herschel stripped. You know men, they like to fool around... Well, who doesn't? So there we were, stark naked, chasing each other in that delicious cool water... There's nothing like doing it under water... Whoooeeee! Ohhhh-hahhh! *(emitting a series of sexual grunts and groans)*

CATHERINE. *(sitting up)* Are you talking to me?

RENNIE. That Herschel...he knows how to pleasure a woman. You know what I mean?

CATHERINE. *(amazed)* You're back! What do you know...?

RENNIE. It's not so much the size of their equipment as its versatility!

CATHERINE. Maybe there's still hope. So, Ren, do you remember the "plan" we were talking about before?

RENNIE. "Plan?"

CATHERINE. Our grand "escape?"

RENNIE. *(excited)* Escape?

47

CATHERINE. Shhhhhh, not so loud. ...Paris? on the QE2?

RENNIE. *(clapping)* Oh Paris! I *love* Paris!

CATHERINE. *(whispering)* But it's got to be a secret. You can't tell a soul. Not even your daughter. Especially not your daughter!

RENNIE. Paris! *(She mimes locking her lips with a key and throwing it away.)* So, when are we going?

CATHERINE. The boat leaves in ten days.

RENNIE. *TEN DAYS?!*

CATHERINE. I raided my secret bank account and booked our tickets. All I have to do now is order a car service to take us to the pier.

RENNIE. Stop, stop! I'm going to wet my pants!

CATHERINE. *(pulling it out from under her pillow)* I've got my passport, so you have to get yours. The trick will be getting out of *here*. I've tried everything – faking heart attacks, slipping out with visitors... You wouldn't have any bright ideas, would you?

RENNIE. About what?

CATHERINE. Our escape plan.

RENNIE. Right... Let me put on my thinking thing.

(A long silence as she he shuts her eyes to think.)

CATHERINE. Rennie? Rennie? Yoo hooooo, anybody home? *(to herself)* What's wrong with you, woman? Like *she'd* be any help!

(more silence)

RENNIE. *(opening her eyes)* I've got it! We create a division.

CATHERINE. A *division?*

RENNIE. You know, when you start a riot like in those jail-break movies.

CATHERINE. A *diversion!*

RENNIE. That's what I said! *(in a conspiratorial whisper)* We take one of the guards hostage or set a little fire on the premises.

CATHERINE. Set a little fire?

RENNIE. And then make a break for it while everyone's distilled.

CATHERINE. You mean, *distracted.*

(**ESPERANZA** *suddenly appears with* **RITA**.)

ESPERANZA. Hey, Miss Popularity, your daughter's here. I've never seen anyone go out as much as you!

RITA. She's a party girl. Always was and always will be! *(kissing* **RENNIE***)* Hi, Ma. *(waving at* **CATHERINE***)* Hi, Cath.

CATHERINE. *(waving back)* Hi, Reets.

ESPERANZA. Don't forget to bring her back now. We love this woman! *(She exits, blowing kisses.)*

RITA. *(to* **RENNIE***)* So, how are you feeling today?

RENNIE. Great! Catherine and I are going to escape!

(**CATHERINE** *groans.*)

RITA. Really? And where are you planning to go?

(a suspenseful silence)

RENNIE. To Abercrombie and Fitch!

RITA. Do tell!

CATHERINE. Thank you, God.

RENNIE. But I need one of those things to get there. What are they called?

RITA. A bus…

RENNIE. No, a passage…a password…a passenger…

RITA. A passport?

RENNIE. That's it, a *passport!*

RITA. Silly girl, you don't need a passport to go shopping. *(looking at her watch)* Oh no, look at the time! If you want to get your hair and nails done, we'd better get moving. The traffic is unbelievable! You two! A person would think you're a couple of four year olds.

(**RENNIE** *puts on a saucy hat.*)

CATHERINE. What a lovely hat!

RENNIE. You like it?

CATHERINE. It's very becoming!

RENNIE. *(taking it off)* Here, it's yours.

CATHERINE. No, I couldn't…

RENNIE. I have so many. I can't possibly wear them all.

CATHERINE. But it's part of your collection!

RENNIE. Collection, erection!

RITA. *Ma!*

RENNIE. Please…I insist! Bend down.

RITA. You'd better take it or you'll hurt her feelings.

CATHERINE. But where will I wear it? I never go out.

RENNIE. *(plopping it on CATHERINE's head)* What about our… Escape!

CATHERINE. To Abercrombie and Fitch!

RENNIE. To Abercrombie and Fitch.

CATHERINE. I try to humor her as much as possible.

RITA. Well Ma, it's time to go.

RENNIE. *(starts spinning around the room in circles)* I want my passport! I want my passport! I want my passport! *(etc. as)*

CATHERINE. Rennie, Rennie, calm down.

RITA. *(voice lowered)* When Dad died, her mind started to go. He was her world. At first, she thought she was the one who'd passed and left *him*! She cooked his favorite meals, wore his favorite outfits, and kept up a steady stream of conversation to console him – "There, there, Rennie just went to the store to pick up a few things. Don't look so sad, she'll be back in a minute." It was heartbreaking! It took her awhile to figure out that *he* was the one who had left *her*. Then things really started to fall apart. She began sneaking out of the house to look for him. Once she disappeared for two days. *Two whole days!* The police finally found her at the bus station, slumped over a toilet in the ladies room, babbling incoherently. Someone had stolen her wheelchair and all her money…

CATHERINE. *(hands over her ears)* Stop, stop…

RITA. That's why we keep dropping by. We're terrified she's going to slip out when no one's looking.

RENNIE. *(still spinning in circles)* I want my passport! I want my passport! *(etc. as...)*

CATHERINE. You wouldn't happen to know where it is, would you?! We play this game, "Passport, passport, who's got their passport?" I have mine. See? *(pulling it out from under her pillow)*

RITA. It must be somewhere at home, I'll look around. *(reaching for CATHERINE's)* May I?

CATHERINE. Be my guest.

RITA. *(opening it)* Ohhh! You look like a movie star!

CATHERINE. Please! I'm a ruin!

RITA. Look at those cheek bones!

RENNIE. Let me see, let me see!

RITA. *(handing it to her)* I'd die for cheekbones like that!

RENNIE. *(engrossed with her picture)* Hubba hubba!

RITA. *(glancing at her watch)* Well, we'd better get moving if you want to make it to the beauty parlor and the Hungry Man diner.
(grabbing another hat) Maybe you'd like to join us next time.

CATHERINE. *(amazed)* Who me?

RENNIE. Yes, come, come!

RITA. *(heading out the door)* Now don't do anything we wouldn't do. *(disappearing down the hall)* The poor thing...she has no one...no one...

CATHERINE. *(Slowly making her way to RENNIE's chaise, wraps herself in one of her shawls, takes off her hat, scoops her hair up into a knot, puts the hat back on and settles down with a sigh.)* My first luncheon invitation since I've been here! I'm dazzled, dazzled! My family has never taken me anywhere. Well, how could they? They're all dead. Except for Royal. *(with a sigh)* Poor Royal, scared of his own shadow, with nothing much to show for himself... Is it my fault? Probably... I wasn't much of a mother...

The only thing I was good at was mixing my colors and slopping paint on the canvas...with brushes... palette knives, even my fingers! Ohh, the smell...the rush... the delirium... I was lost in another world. I got what I deserved... Why should he care about me? What did I ever do for him? Took him skating on the Charles a few times and that was pretty much it. He was a wonderful skater though, flying over the ice on that glittering edge... Enough, enough... Count your blessings... At least you've got a roof over your head... *(catching her reflection in the mirror)* and this attractive new hat. It was very generous of her to give it to me... Poor thing, always crying out for that dreadful Herschel she's so fond of. Well, they were happy together... How many couples can you say that about? Two? Two and a half, at the most! *(pause)* Out! Out! I want out!

(**RITA** *and* **RENNIE** *reappear.*)

CATHERINE. *(jumping up)* You're back!

RITA. *(heading towards* **RENNIE**'*s night table and grabbing a pill bottle)* We forgot her nitroglycerin. You never know.

RENNIE. That hat looks so much better on you than me.

RITA. *(heading into the bathroom)* Since we're too late for the beauty parlor, I may as well duck into the bathroom. "A bird in the hand is worth two in the bush." *(She exits.)*

RENNIE. *(grabbing* **CATHERINE**'*s arm)* Come on, let's go!

CATHERINE. Where?

RENNIE. You know – our *escape hatch!* I've got the matches right here.

CATHERINE. Where did you get those?

RENNIE. From Herschel. I keep begging him to stop smoking, but it's hopeless.

CATHERINE. *(snatching them out of her hands)* Quick, give them to me! We're not doing this now, but later next week!

RENNIE. *Let's burn the place to the ground!*

CATHERINE. No! We'll just set a little fire!

RENNIE. *Wipe it off the face of the earth!*

CATHERINE. We don't want to hurt anyone. We just want to set off the smoke alarm so we can slip out in the ensuing melée.

RENNIE. *And let all the prisoners escape!*

CATHERINE. Now, listen: you've got to remember to ask your daughter for your passport.

RENNIE. My passport...

CATHERINE. You won't be able to board the ship without it.

RENNIE. I won't be able to board the ship without it...

CATHERINE. *(handing her a nearby pen)* So, I want you to write "passport" on your hand.

RENNIE. Wait! I know! Let's prick our fingers and make a blood pact. That's what Rachel and I used to do! *(removing a hat pin and holding it aloft) I* never forget a blood pact, never! *(plunging it into her finger)* Ah!

CATHERINE. What on earth?

RENNIE. Now give me yours.

> (**CATHERINE** *holds a finger out* **RENNIE** *pricks it.* **CATHERINE** *gasps.*)

RENNIE. Done! Now press your finger against mine so our blood mixes and swear... *(pause)* What is it we're swearing again?

CATHERINE. Don't forget your passport.

RENNIE. Right... Don't forget your passport. *(pressing her finger against* **CATHERINE***'s)* Now say it together...

CATHERINE & RENNIE. Don't forget your passport.

RITA. *(emerging from the bathroom)* I'm back! Miss me?

End of Scene

Scene Eight

*(Four days later, around five in the afternoon. Arts
and crafts class in the sun room.* **MARIE CLAIRE,** *their
sexy French teacher has gathered everyone around a
picture window so they can do watercolors of the park
below. Those in attendance are* **RENNIE, IRIS, HENRY,
SHERWOOD,** *(who's fallen asleep) and* **CATHERINE,**
*wearing a terrifying looking pair of magnifying
glasses, intent on painting* **IRIS.** *An unusual calm has
descended. All we hear is the whisper of brushes across
the page, except for* **CATHERINE** *who works with consid-
erably more gusto.* **MARIE CLAIRE** *walks among them
looking at their work. As the scene progresses, the sky
darkens and a storm rolls in.)*

MARIE CLAIRE. Nice work, class... *Très bien!* Show us what
you see when you go to the park. Is it the blowing
trees, the shadows on the ground or the patterns of
the people down below? Art celebrates your point of
view, what you see and feel, so make it personal. *A
vous! (pausing to look at* **CATHERINE***'s work) Mon dieu,
quelle horreur!*

CATHERINE. Yes, I'm focusing on Iris today! It's rather
clever isn't it? I particularly like the chair sprouting
out of her head. It adds a certain...*je ne sais quoi!*

ESPERANZA. *A chacuns ses goûts...*

CATHERINE. To each his own, indeed! My "Portraits of the
Damned."

*(**SHERWOOD** begins to snore.)*

MARIE CLAIRE. *(tapping him on the shoulder)* Wake up, *Cheri...*

SHERWOOD. *(waking with a start)* Who? What? Where am I?

MARIE CLAIRE. You're in art class now.

SHERWOOD. *(trying to grab her)* I was just dreaming about
you! Kiss me, you Minx!

MARIE CLAIRE. *(in French:) ATTENTION, SHERWOOD, SOIS
SAGE!*

SHERWOOD. *(fumbling with his fly)* Let Sherwood show you how much he loves you!

MARIE CLAIRE. *(snatching his hands)* If you don't behave, you'll have to be taken back to your room!

SHERWOOD. *(starting to cry)* I'm sorry, don't be mad. Don't be mad. Please don't be mad!

MARIE CLAIRE. I'm not mad, *mon chou,* just try and remember where you are.

HENRY. Help! Help! Someone help me please! I need help! Help! Help! Please help me! *(overlapping)*

IRIS. *(singing)* "Hi ho the dairy-oh, the farmer in the sink!

RENNIE. *(to* **MARIE CLAIRE***)* Catherine and I are making a break for it.

MARIE CLAIRE. Where are you going?

CATHERINE. Out! Out! I want out!

RENNIE. *(joining her)* Out! Out! We want out!

HENRY & IRIS. *(joining them)* Out! Out! We want out! Out! Out! We want out! *(etc.)*

(**CATHERINE** *starts banging her paint brush against her water glass.*)

ALL THE PATIENTS. *(also banging on things)* Out! Out! We want out! Out! Out! We want out!

MARIE CLAIRE. Class! Class! *S'il vous plait.*

CHARLES. *(rushing in)* What's going on in here?

MARIE CLAIRE. They want out.

CHARLES. I want out. You want out. Everyone in their right mind wants out of here! *(He starts conducting them.)*

MARIE CLAIRE. Charles? What's come over you?

CHARLES. Fatigue, sweetheart. Good old fashioned burn out. Out! Out! I want out!

THE PATIENTS. Out! Out! We want out! Out! Out! We want out!

MARIE CLAIRE. If one of the nurses saw this, you'd be fired.

CHARLES & THE PATIENTS. *(louder still)* Out! Out! We want out! Out! Out! Out! We want out!

MARIE CLAIRE. *Assez, assez, calmez-vous!*

CHARLES. I, for one, would rather be flying my little plane over those misty Hawaiian islands – Kauai, Oahu, Molokai, Lanai, Maui…

HENRY. Me, I dream of returning to the fertile crescent, the cradle of Western civilization as we know it.

ALL. *(astonished) Henry?*

HENRY. All I have to do is shut my eyes and I can see it as clear as day…The orchards, valleys and Tigris-Euphrates…I was an archeologist, a digger. I ran more than nineteen excavations over there. And what was the most amazing artifact I ever unearthed, you ask? *(lowering his voice)* Clusters of bronze bells dating back to the time when cavemen rode three toed horses across the plains. The actual bells were small… no bigger than ping pong balls, but so clotted with debris it took us three full weeks to clean them… But what made them so remarkable was the disconnect between their dainty shape and the thunderous sound they made – like ten ton church bells calling the faithful to prayer. Those babies peeled hosannas that shook the skies clear up to heaven and back. I became obsessed with them and would leave camp under cover of night to ring them, alone… You see, their music wasn't meant for human ears. The first time I shook them, the sky grew dark with birds. Hundreds and hundreds of ancient birds – *pterodactyls!* They appeared out of nowhere and started to sing, but not the usual caws and whistles you'd expect, but *words!* You've never heard anything like it! Flying dinosaurs singing actual *lyrics!* I couldn't understand them because it was a language I didn't know, but the air suddenly reverberated with these majestic choruses… I felt this rush of…I don't know…peace, acceptence, surrender… For a moment I felt myself lifting off the ground…

(He takes a string of bells out of his pocket and rings them. They make a mystical far away sound. The room starts to darken.)

CATHERINE. *(in a whisper)* I hear them.

SHERWOOD. Me too!

RENNIE. *(swooning)* I'm going to die!

MARIE CLAIRE. *C'est comme un rêve...*

CHARLES. *(reaching for the bells)* May I?

HENRY. *(handing them to him)* Be my guest.

CHARLES. *(shaking them with brio)* Come on fellas, bring on those nasty birds!

(Nothing happens.)

HENRY. That's the problem, once they were taken from their homeland, they lost their power.

CATHERINE. Not unlike some other ancient relics I know...

RENNIE. *(to MARIE CLAIRE)* Catherine and I are running away, but don't tell anyone, it's a secret.

CHARLES. Take me with you!

MARIE-CLAIRE. *Charles?!*

RENNIE. *(in a whisper)* But don't tell, it's a secret.

CHARLES. Not a word. I only know of one person who ever made it out of a home. My daddy.

CATHERINE. How did he do it?

CHARLES. He dressed up as a maintenance man and just shuffled out the front door. A raggedy old black man... No one looked twice.

CATHERINE. And where did he go?

CHARLES. He'd made and lost a fortune at the track so he took off to South America, which has the fastest race horses in the world. He sent us a bunch of postcards from Buenos Aires and that was the last we ever heard of him... I know I shouldn't say this out loud, but anyone who jumps over the fence is a hero in my book.

CATHERINE. Mine too!

MARIE CLAIRE. Keep this up, and I'll have to report you!

CATHERINE. And where would *you* go after you clear that fence?

CHARLES. *(grabbing* **MARIE CLAIRE***)* To Maui with her!

MARIE CLAIRE. *(pleased, but feigning resistance)* Charles!

CHARLES. Hey, sweet thing, let's get out of here while our equipment still works. *(He plants a juicy kiss on her lips.)*

MARIE CLAIRE. *(half heartedly struggling to get away)* What do you think you're...

SHERWOOD. Go! Go! Go! *(etc.)*

THE OTHER PATIENTS. *(joining him)* Go! Go! Go! Go! *(etc., as...)*

IRIS. The summer house, the summer house! It happened in the summer house!

CHARLES. *(pushing* **MARIE-CLAIRE** *into a corner)* I burn for you, baby and you know it!

MARIE CLAIRE. *(softly)* What's gotten into you? You're a married man!

CATHERINE. Oh please! All husbands cheat on their wives! Mine included, but not with other women, he only had eyes for himself. He was lover *and* belovèd, wrapped into one. It was that wretched Lowell blood, thinned to the point of evaporation... My star was rising, while his was drowning in a martini glass. When he finally sobered up, it was too late... He caught me once. *(lowering her voice)* In our bedroom, no less. There I was, *in flagrante delicto* with one of my young art students... Oh, I was baaaaad!

RENNIE. *(applauding with glee)* Whooooeeee!

CHARLES. My kind of woman!

(There's a sudden crack of thunder. Everyone jumps as rain starts to pelt the windows. The room darkens more.)

HENRY.	**SHERWOOD.**	**IRIS.**
Help! Help! Somebody help me please! I need help!	Jesus Christ, what was that?	OH NO, MY HANDS FELL OFF! JELLY, JELLY, JELLY!

MARIE CLAIRE. Alright, class, just take it easy until the storm passes.

RENNIE. *(to* CATHERINE, *pulling a passport out of her pocket)* Pssst, Catherine! Look what Herschel found. I've been meaning to give it to you.

CATHERINE. *(snatching it)* You got it!

CHARLES. Going somewhere?

CATHERINE. *(with a hula-like flourish)* Wouldn't you like to know!

End of Scene

Scene Nine

(Six days later, around 10 am. Catherine and Rennie's room. Their escape is on. RENNIE's ready to go, all dolled up in one of her outfits. CATHERINE, still in her nightgown, is flying around the room filling a beat up leather satchel with their pills and personal effects.)

CATHERINE. I've got to trust you about what's in these bottles since I can't read the labels.

RENNIE. Just don't forget the pink ones for pain.

CATHERINE. *(handing her a bottle)* What color are these? They're so small I can't see them.

RENNIE. *(opening it and pouring out a few)* Green!

CATHERINE. What are they for?

RENNIE. Beats me.

CATHERINE. Do they look familiar?

RENNIE. Nope. They must be yours.

CATHERINE. I don't take green pills.

RENNIE. Are you sure?

CATHERINE. I'm told mine are white, blue, maroon and purple.

RENNIE. Then throw 'em out!

CATHERINE. *(tossing them in a wastepaper basket)* Done! *(handing her another bottle)* What about these?

RENNIE. What about them?

CATHERINE. Can you make out what it says on the label?

RENNIE. *(squinting at it)* Not a word.

CATHERINE. *(shaking it)* They sound serious.

RENNIE. They *do* sound serious. Toss 'em in the bag!

CATHERINE. *(She does, then hands her another bottle.)* What about these?

RENNIE. Shake 'em.

(CATHERINE *does.*)

RENNIE. Those sound really serious! Toss 'em in!

CATHERINE. I'm so afraid I might miss something important. Like your heart medicine. You do take heart medicine, don't you?

RENNIE. I don't remember.

CATHERINE. *(shaking another bottle which sounds different from the others)* What's this? It sounds like a silver dollar!

RENNIE. Shake it. *(CATHERINE does.)* Quick, throw it out!

(She does.)

RENNIE. Wait a minute, wait a minute, we're forgetting the most important thing of all!

CATHERINE. What?

RENNIE. *Stool softener!*

CATHERINE & RENNIE. *(grabbing their respective bottles)* Stool softener! Stool softener! Stool softener!

RENNIE. Woa, that was close!

CATHERINE. Don't even go there!

RENNIE. This is fun!

CATHERINE. This *is* fun!

(RENNIE strikes a flamenco pose and starts humming the Toreador tune from "Carmen" as she throws the bottle into her bag. CATHERINE joins in with a few yelps, and high spirited flamenco moves of her own.)

CHARLES. *(knocking on the door)* Everything all right in there?

CATHERINE. Right as rain! We're just greeting the new day.

(waiting to hear him leave)

RENNIE. *(whispered)* Now what?

CATHERINE. I've got to get dressed.

RENNIE. But you never get dressed.

CATHERINE. You don't expect me to board the QE2 looking like this! I had Royal bring me some of my old clothes for the occasion. *(pause)* What time is it?

RENNIE. Noon-ish?

CATHERINE. Good God, we've got to get a wiggle on! *(Grabbing her wardrobe bag and hat, she heads towards the bathroom, then stops.)* Could I borrow a lipstick? Not that I'll be able to see what I'm doing…

RENNIE. *(handing her a cosmetic bag)* Take whatever you want.

CATHERINE. Just pray we'll be able to slip past the front desk.

RENNIE. *(bowing her head)* "*Baruch Atah Adonai Eloheinu…*"

CATHERINE. *(going into the bathroom and shutting the door)* Atta girl, keep it up.

RENNIE. "*Melech Haolam Ashher Kidshanu Bemitzvotav Vetzivanu…*" Wait a minute, what am I praying for again?

CATHERINE. *(from the bathroom)* A smooth getaway.

RENNIE. Right, right… "*Lehadlik Ner Shell Shabbat.*"

SHERWOOD. Nurse, nurse!

RENNIE. Amen.

(The hall noisily comes to life in the distance.)

SHERWOOD. I'm ready for my bath. I'm naked and waiting for you.

IRIS. And so all the pretty parasols explode.

HENRY. Help. Help. I need help.

RENNIE. This is the noisiest hotel I've ever been in.

HENRY, SHERWOOD & IRIS. NURSE! NURSE! HELP! NURSE!

RENNIE. Why is everyone calling for a nurse? This isn't a hospital, it's hotel! The Four Star Mount Airy Hotel! Hotels don't have nurses, but everyone keeps yelling for them as if they're all over the place. So maybe it is a hospital and not a hotel! But it can't be a hospital because it's too noisy for a hospital and doesn't smell like one. In fact it smells worse. But nothing smells worse than a hospital except for a…except for a… *(pause)* Oh no… It couldn't be a…couldn't be a…be a….

HENRY. *(under)* Help! Help! Someone help me please! I need help! Help! Help! Please help me!

IRIS. *(under)* I said, "It's *your* turn to change the baby!"

SHERWOOD. Nurse! Nurse! I need a nurse! I'm dying for love!

RENNIE. *(under)* A nursing home, could it? Nursing homes are where old people are taken to die! Herschel promised we'd never end up in one, he *promised!*

IRIS. The globe eaters defy gravity every time!

RENNIE. *Herschel, where the hell are you? I haven't seen you in so long, a person would think you'd died!* Oh my God, I think you *did* die. You died in your sleep at the hospital. Last time I visited you, your bed was empty. *Herschel? Where did I go after you went away? Did I do something bad? Was I a bad girl? Did you put me in a nursing home because I was a bad girl?*

(IRIS, HENRY and SHERWOOD's chorus reaches a crescendo.)

Help! Help! I've got to get the hell out of here! Catherine! Catherine! Catherine?!

(Silence. CATHERINE emerges from the bathroom, transformed – unrecognizable in a lovely dress, hair swept up in a Gibson knot, crowned with the hat RENNIE gave her.)

CATHERINE. Enter the Queen!

RENNIE. Catherine? What did you do with Catherine?

CATHERINE. Easy, easy, it's me.

RENNIE. What did you do with Catherine?

CATHERINE. I'm Catherine, your roommate!

RENNIE. *(gazing at her)* Roommate?

CATHERINE. Listen carefully and repeat after me. We're going to create a diversion.

RENNIE. "We're going to create a diversion."

CATHERINE. We're going to get out the good old matches.

RENNIE. "We're going to get out the good old matches."

CATHERINE. We're going to set a small fire on the premises.

RENNIE. *And burn the fucking place down to the ground!*

CATHERINE. No, just set off the smoke alarm so we can slip out during the ensuing melée.

RENNIE. "Slip out during the ensuing melée"…

CATHERINE. But you have to do it since I can't see the matches.

RENNIE. "But you have to do it since I can't see the matches."

CATHERINE. No, *you* have to do it, since *I* can't see the matches!

RENNIE. "No, *you* have to do it, since *I* can't see the matches!"

CATHERINE. Stop repeating everything I say and just listen to me. *(slowly)* I'm the one who's blind, so *you* have to set the fire.

RENNIE. I have to set the fire!

CATHERINE. Good girl! *(placing a small bag on her lap and then covering it with a shawl)* And here are some extra things I packed for our…you know…voyage.

ESPERANZA. *(suddenly entering)* There's a car service here for you Miss Rennie… *(noticing* **CATHERINE***)* My, don't you look grand. Where are you going? To the rec room for hot date with Henry?

CATHERINE. Dream on! To the New York Botanical Garden. Her sister Lady Rachel Bachelor just flew in from London. She's an avid gardener, and wants to give us a tour, so she sent a car to pick us up. You should see her roses…

RENNIE. *(in an English accent)* "The most heavenly shade of pink."

CATHERINE. *(likewise)* "Like Bonnie Prince Charles' blushing bottom when he popped out of his mummy's womb."

ESPERANZA. Well, this is the first I heard about any trip to the botanical gardens, so I better give your son a call to make sure he knows about it. *(She exits.)*

RENNIE. Oh, God. Oh, God. Now what?

CATHERINE. We board in less than an hour.

RENNIE. Board?

CHARLES. *(suddenly knocking and entering)* That car service is still waiting for you, Miss Rennie. Whoa. Look at you. What's going on?

CATHERINE.	RENNIE.
Excuse me, Charles, but don't you knock before you enter?	We're meeting my sister Rachel at the New York Botanical thing.

CHARLES. One at a time, please. One. At a time.

CATHERINE. We're meeting her sister at the New York Botanical Garden. She sent us her car.

CHARLES. This is news to me. Does Esperanza know?

CATHERINE. Of course she knows! That woman knows everything!

CHARLES. Something smells fishy.

CATHERINE. I'm finally going on my first outing and you call that *fishy*. Oh, I get it! It makes your life easier if I just lie here like some rotting carcass on the side of the road. That way you can keep an eye on me.

CHARLES. OK ladies, what's going on? And what are those suspicious bags you're trying to hide in your lap?

RENNIE. Excuse me, but I thought female patients had a right to their privacy. You're trespassing in my…*boudoir*, as it were. I happen to have intimate toiletries in here…dainty private things you have no right to see, let alone handle.

CHARLES. Sorry, sorry.

CATHERINE. This is my first outing, Charles, I'm frightened…so indulge a doddering old lady for once, let her bring a few things along.

CHARLES. Tell you what, Miss Catherine, let me give your son a call to make sure he knows about this.

CATHERINE. Charles!

CHARLES. Yes?

CATHERINE. Here goes nothing…that is to say, everything. You've always struck me as a man of conviction. Someone who's moved by his heart, not his head.

CHARLES. Well, you got that right!

CATHERINE. Remember how you said everyone in their right mind wants out of here? Remember how you said you'd like to be flying your plane over those Hawaiian islands? *(RENNIE starts doing hula moves as...)* Remember your father? And remember how you said anyone who jumps over the fence is a hero in your book? *(pause)* Well, *do* you?

CHARLES. *(catching on)* Oh no you don't...

CATHERINE. Oh yes, I do...

CHARLES. Oh boy...

CATHERINE. That's right... Oh boy!

CHARLES. Oh boy, oh boy, oh boy!

RENNIE. Oh boy, oh boy, oh boy, oh boy!

(a tense silence)

CHARLES. I'll lose my job if I let you get away with this.

CATHERINE. But then you'll be free to fly over your dreaming islands. *Free!*

RENNIE. *(more hula moves)* Come to Mamma!

CHARLES. Walk out the door into the cockpit of my buddy's little Cessna? Life doesn't work that way.

CATHERINE. Unless you seize it by the tail. As the wise man said: "Leap, and the net will appear."

(silence)

It will, Charles! Look at your father!

(Silence as he considers.)

CHARLES. And where are you headed, if I may ask?

CATHERINE. *(grabbing the handles of RENNIE's wheel chair)* Just the New York Botanical Garden, and we'd better get a wiggle on before that car takes off without us. Whoops, I forgot something.

(CATHERINE makes her way back to their room, strikes a match, drops it in her wastebasket and grabs her hat as...)

RENNIE. *(taking* **CHARLES**' *hands and kissing them)* Charles, Charles, you're such a mensch. My kind of guy... I had a dream about you the other night... Where were we? On top of the Eiffel Tower! Just you and me, tossing a beachball back and forth.

CATHERINE. *(returns, waving her hat)* I can't be seen in public without this! *(then resumes pushing* **RENNIE***)*

RENNIE. Atta girl, keeping going, then hang a left past the front desk...

CATHERINE. *A bientôt, chère* Charles... We'll be back in time for supper.

CHARLES. *(to himself)* Somehow I find that hard to believe.

RENNIE. Hasta la vista, baby!

CHARLES. *(watching them go)* Bon voyage! Au revoir! Arividerchi! Auf wiedersehen! Dasvidania! Off you go! I wasn't cut out for this kind of work – all that screaming, crying and mopping up. It's like you're being punished for something, but you didn't do nothing' 'cept get old. It ain't your fault! You were just minding your own business getting on with your life – celebrating birthdays and anniversaries, playing with the grandkids, then blam...! You have a couple of strokes and it's, "Welcome to Mount Airy! Have a nice day!" This is it for me. I've had it! I'm outta here. *You go girls! Pick some of those daisies for me!*

(He exits. We hear a car door slam and wheels accelerating in the distance.)

End of Scene

Scene Ten

(Two hours later. **CATHERINE** *and* **RENNIE** *are spread out in deck chairs on the upper deck of the QE2 in a blaze of sunlight. They're almost unrecognizable, sporting sunglasses and fluttering scarves. They're dizzy with excitement, waiting for the ship to set sail. An elegant steward from Trinidad hovers nearby.)*

STEWARD. *(approaching with a stack of blankets)* Would either of you charming young ladies like a blanket? We'll be encountering some stiff winds once we set sail.

CATHERINE. *(in an English accent)* Please!

(He covers **CATHERINE** *'s legs and tucks in her feet.)*

RENNIE. I just love Atlantic City! You remembered to pack suntan lotion, didn't you? I burn like a son of a bitch!

CATHERINE. *(to the* **STEWARD***)* Thank you so much, that was frightfully thoughtful of you.

STEWARD. *(with a little bow)* My pleasure.

RENNIE. *(to* **CATHERINE***)* Maybe we can take a little dip after lunch.

STEWARD. *(approaching* **RENNIE** *with a blanket)* And for you, my lady?

RENNIE. Why not!

(He covers **RENNIE** *'s legs and feet with a flourish.)*

RENNIE. *(to* **CATHERINE***)* I've always loved the service at these old Boardwalk hotels.

CATHERINE. To my mind, no one can beat the service at the Ritz. *Numero quinze, Place Vandôme.*

RENNIE. *(in a whisper)* Why are you talking like that?

CATHERINE. Because I'm feeling very grand. So grand, in fact, that I'm thinking of *becoming* Lady Rachel Bachelor on this journey. *(To the steward:)* I say young man, my sister and I are parched and would enjoy a spot of that heavenly smelling bouillon you were passing around awhile ago. It *is* beef bouillon, isn't it? I don't see as well as I used to.

STEWARD. Indeed it is, my Lady. *(offering her a cup)* May I?

CATHERINE. Why, thank you. Though I'd be happier if you addressed me as Lady Rachel Bachelor.

STEWARD. Then, Lady Rachel Bachelor, it is! *(offering* **RENNIE** *some bouillon)* And for you, Madame?

RENNIE. *(taking it)* Let 'er rip!

CATHERINE. *(to the* **STEWARD**, *getting giddier by the minute)* What a day! Perfect for a picnic, *en plein air,* don't you think?

STEWARD. *Une bonne journée!*

CATHERINE. *(flirtatiously)* Perhaps you'd care to join us for a spot of wine and soupçon of paté in our stateroom a bit later.

STEWARD. I wish I could Lady Bachelor, but alas we do have our rules. *(He moves to another part of the deck.)*

(The captain of the ship suddenly appears, tentatively approaching **CATHERINE.***)*

THE CAPTAIN. *(with a creamy English accent)* Excuse me for bothering you, Madame, but might you be Catherine Sargent? I noticed her name among our first class passengers that are sailing with us today and thought you might be she.

CATHERINE. *(panicking)* You found me!

THE CAPTAIN. *(taking her hand and kissing it)* I'm dazzled, quite undone! It's a pleasure to have you with us.

CATHERINE. Why thank you. I'm amazed you recognized me.

THE CAPTAIN. Dear lady, let me introduce myself, I'm Sir Reginald Allen Pointer, the third, captain of the ship and your greatest fan!

CATHERINE. Please!

THE CAPTAIN. Returning to your old stamping grounds are you?

CATHERINE. You got it!

THE CAPTAIN. Ah, Paris...

CATHERINE. Paris.

RENNIE. *Paris?*

(*Silence as they smile at each other.*)

THE CAPTAIN. Please forgive me for intruding, but I've always wanted to meet you and hope you and your companion will join me at my table one evening?

CATHERINE.	RENNIE.
Why thank you, that's very kind.	Yes, yes, yes, yes, Yes!

THE CAPTAIN. Until then. And on behalf of the entire crew – from our muscle-bound stevedores, to our French chefs, Viennese dance instructors and resident astronomers – I wish you a most delightful voyage.

(**CATHERINE** *and* **RENNIE** *swoon, as he exits. Silence.*)

CATHERINE. (*grabbing* **RENNIE**'s *arm*) Look at us! We did it, we did it!

RENNIE. Did what?

CATHERINE. Escaped from that wretched nursing home! (*pause*) You were brilliant…

RENNIE. I was?

CATHERINE. *Brilliant!* (*She sings a loud exultant note.*)

(*The ship's horn suddenly gives a mighty blast.*)

RENNIE. What was that?

CATHERINE. The ship's horn.

RENNIE. What ship?

CATHERINE. The ship we're on…the QE2!

RENNIE. Oh my God, the buildings are moving! *The buildings are moving!*

CATHERINE. They're not moving, *we* are!

RENNIE. Where are we going?

CATHERINE. On a great adventure!

RENNIE. Great Adventure, I love amusement parks! Especially the roller floater!

CATHERINE. *Coaster!* Roller *coaster!*

RENNIE. The higher, the better!

CATHERINE. Up we go... Hold on tight...

(The ship's horn blasts again, setting off a wave of cheers and tooting horns.)

RENNIE. Do you hear people cheering?

CATHERINE. Loud and clear.

RENNIE. And horns tooting?

CATHERINE. That too!

RENNIE. *(in ecstasies)* Are we in the first car?

CATHERINE. Right up front!

RENNIE. Ohhh, I'm going to die!

CATHERINE. Now buckle yourself in, I don't want to lose you!

RENNIE. Look out belowwwwww!

CATHERINE. And we're off!

(They raise their arms preparing for the plunge as a blizzard of confetti falls from above. The lights start to close around them as...)

(THE CURTAIN SLOWLY FALLS.)

Also by
Tina Howe...

Approaching Zanzibar

The Art of Dining

Birth and After Birth

Coastal Disturbances

Museum

One Shoe Off

Painting Churches

Pride's Crossing

Shrinking Violets and Towering Tiger Lilies

OTHER TITLES AVAILABLE FROM SAMUEL FRENCH

SHRINKING VIOLETS AND TOWERING TIGER LILIES

Tina Howe

Seven Brief Plays About Women in Distress

To go through life as a woman is to be in distress most of the time, so these short plays alight on situations that are inherently distressing – doctor visits, photo shoots, looking for the right dress and navigating around swimming pools. Since we're blessed with uncanny reserves of strength and imagination, we tend to emerge triumphant. One way or another these are comedies about transformation.

Appearances - *(2f)* set in the ladies' dressing room of a department store. A mousy woman hoping to be the belle of the ball tries on dress after dress, exhausting the patience of the woman in charge of the area.

The Divine Fallacy - *(1m, 1f)* set in a photographer's studio. A camera-shy novelist needs a head shot for her upcoming novel. Chaos ensues during her photo shoot with a suave fashion photographer.

Through a Glass Darkly - *(1m, 1f)* set in an optometrist's office. Things spin out of control when a young playwright visits her optometrist for an emergency eye exam.

Teeth - *(1m, 1f)* set in a dentist's office. It's Bach's birthday. A neurotic woman has come to her dentist to have a filling replaced, but he's struggling with his own problems.

Water Music - *(1m, 2f)* set in the pool area of a health club. Ophelia unexpectedly pops up in the whirlpool of a health club after having drowned in "Hamlet", creating havoc for the lifeguard and a retired school teacher.

Milk and Water - *(6f)* set in a pool. The Nursing Mothers' Water Aerobics class is waiting for their teacher to show up. When she cancels, they take over the class with stunning results.

Skin Deep - *(2m, 1f)* set on the R train in New York City. Daphne, the wood nymph is being chased through the subway system by Apollo. She flies into the arms of an infamous dermatologist who tries to save her. But can he?

OTHER TITLES AVAILABLE FROM SAMUEL FRENCH

THE ART OF DINING

Tina Howe

Comedy / 3m, 6f / Interior

Cal and Ellen are the owners and sole staff of a small, elegant gourmet restaurant. Cal's main preoccupation is paying back the $75,000 it cost to start it up, and that means packing in the customers. Chef Ellen is preoccupied with the food's quality and stopping Cal from sampling the ingredients. The diners act out their own private dramas over dinner and their conversations are exquisite burlesques of contemporary attitudes. There's a sensual middle aged couple who go into paroxysms of ecstasy just reading the menu and then there's three crass chic young career women. Finally, there's Elizabeth, a maladroit, shy and neurotic writer who's dining with her prospective publisher. Her actions and conversation are unintentionally hilarious and a delicious example of how not to act and what not to talk about while dining.

"A spicy compote of social satire, slapstick zaniness, sight gags and the funniest play I've seen in a long time."
– *Village Voice*

OTHER TITLES AVAILABLE FROM SAMUEL FRENCH

COASTAL DISTURBANCES

Tina Howe

Comedy / 3m, 4f, 2 children (1m, 1f) / Exterior

A Broadway hit which gave Annette Bening and Tim Daly early stage roles, this charming ensemble play follows four generations of vacationers on a Massachusetts beach, focusing on a romance between a lifeguard and a kooky young photographer.

"Generously illuminates the intimate landscape between men and women."
– *The New York Times*

"Enchanting."
– *The New Yorker*

"Endearing."
– NBC TV

"Will appeal only to play goers who like charming and sympathetic characters, tender romance, laughs and rueful wisdom about the pitfalls of love."
– *Variety*

"Whosoever's heart this play does not break, whosoever's soul it does not enthrall, may just lack those organs."
– *New York Magazine*

OTHER TITLES AVAILABLE FROM SAMUEL FRENCH

BIRTH AND AFTER BIRTH

Tina Howe

Comedy / 3m, 2f / Interior

Newly revised! Recently produced in 2006 at the Atlantic Theatre Company in New York City, this witty and sophisticated satire by the author of One Shoe Off and other popular comedies, this play takes place during a child's fourth birthday party. The boy's parents have invited another couple, anthropologists renowned for their international studies of childhood behavior. The adults become so involved in debating various theories of child rearing and telling each other stories that they forget to actually be parents.

"A stunning theatrical experience that explores the magic and madness in family dynamics."
– *Main Line Times*

"An antic farce and a poignant drama...that is laugh out loud funny and disturbingly sober...It's a pearl."
– *Metropolitan D.C. Times*

"One of [Tina Howe's] significant works...Will be remembered as the high point of Philadelphia's annual Theatre Week."
– *TheatreWeek*

OTHER TITLES AVAILABLE FROM SAMUEL FRENCH

PAINTING CHURCHES

Tina Howe

Dramatic Comedy / 1m, 2f / Interior

Gardner and Fanny Church are preparing to move out of their Beacon Hill house to their summer cottage on Cape Cod. Gardner, once a famous poet, now is retired. He slips in and out of senility as his wife Fanny valiantly tries to keep them both afloat. They have asked their daughter, Mags, to come home and help them move. Mags agrees, for she hopes as well to finally paint their portrait. She is now on the verge of artistic celebrity herself and hopes, by painting her parents, to come to terms with them and they with her. Mags triumphs in the end as Fanny and Gardner actually step through the frame and become a work of art ineffable and timeless.

"Beautifully written...A theatrical family portrait that has the shimmer and depth of Renoir portraits."
– *The New York Times*

"A radiant, loving and zestfully humorous play...distinctly Chekhovian. Howe captures the same edgy surface of false hilarity, the same unutterable sadness beneath it, and the indomitable valor beneath both."
– *Time*